UNDER THE MOON

THE UNPUBLISHED EARLY POETRY

BY

William Butler Yeats

EDITED BY

GEORGE BORNSTEIN

S C R I B N E R

New York   London   Toronto   Sydney   Tokyo   Singapore

SCRIBNER
Rockefeller Center
1230 Avenue of the Americas
New York, NY 10020

SCRIBNER is a
trademark of Simon & Schuster Inc.

Designed by Hyun Joo Kim

Manufactured in the United States of America

1   3   5   7   9   10   8   6   4   2

Library of Congress Cataloging-in-Publication Data
Yeats, W. B. (William Butler), 1865–1939.
Under the moon : the unpublished early poetry /
by William Butler Yeats ; edited by George Bornstein.
p.   cm.
Includes bibliographical references.
I. Bornstein, George.   II. Title.
PR5904.U5   1995
821'.8—dc20   95–8445
CIP
ISBN: 0-684-80254-6

To Anne, Michael, and Gráinne Yeats

CONTENTS

INTRODUCTION: Becoming W. B. Yeats   9

NOTES TO INTRODUCTION   23

NOTE ON THE TEXTS   27

POEMS OF THE 1880s   31

    1. *A flower has blossomed*   33

    2. *A double moon or more ago*   34

    3. *Behold the man*   35

    4. *Sir Roland*   36

    5. *Sansloy—Sansfoy—Sansjoy*   51

    6. *The Priest of Pan*   52

    7. *The Magpie*   53

    8. *'Mong meadows of sweet grain*   55

    9. *I heard a rose on the brim*   56

    10. *Hushed in the vale of Dagestan*   57

    11. *For clapping hands*   59

    12. *An Old and Solitary One*   60

13. *The Veiled Voices and the Questions of the Dark*   61

14. *A soul of the fountain*   62

15. *Cyprian*   64

16. *My song thou knowest*   65

17. *The world is but a strange romance*   66

18. *The Old Grey Man*   67

19. *The Dell*   68

20. *Inscription for a Christmas Card*   69

21. *Tower wind-beaten grim*   70

22. *Sunrise*   72

23. *Pan*   74

24. *Child's Play*   75

25. *I sat upon a high gnarled root*   77

26. *The dew comes dropping*   79

27. *The Outlaw's Bridal*   80

28. *Love's Decay*   84

29. *Wherever in the wastes*   89

POEMS OF THE 1890S   91

30. *The Watch-Fire*   93

31. *To a Sister of the Cross and the Rose*   94

32. *The Pathway*   95

33. *He who bids*   96

34. *A Dream of a Life Before This One*   97

35. *He treads a road*   98

36. *On a Child's Death*   99

37. *I will not in grey hours*   100

38. *Though loud years come*   101

NOTES TO THE POEMS   103

INTRODUCTION:
BECOMING W. B. YEATS

Under the Moon makes available for the first time in book form reading texts of thirty-eight unpublished early poems by the major modern poet W. B. Yeats.[1] They span the crucial period during which Yeats remade himself from the unknown and insecure young student Willie Yeats to the more public literary, cultural, and even political figure W. B. Yeats whom we know today. The first poems belong to the early 1880s, preceding his initial publication of verse in the *Dublin University Review* in 1885. They continue through the late 1880s when he assembled his first poetic collection, *The Wanderings of Oisin and Other Poems* (1889), a volume that won numerous reviews but few sales. The last nine poems belong to the early 1890s, when Yeats worked on his second poetic volume, *The Countess Kathleen and Various Legends and Lyrics* (1892). One of them, "A Dream of a Life Before This One," got as far as being set in proof before Yeats canceled it there, presumably because of its biographical frankness about the vexed relationship with his then beloved, Maud

Gonne. The final few lyrics belong to the elaborate manuscript books, one of them a love token for Gonne, that Yeats constructed before the appearance of his first collected edition, the *Poems* (1895) volume, at the age of thirty. When the manuscripts begin, Yeats was a private figure, a talented and sensitive adolescent. By the time that they end, he had become a public figure, already recognized both at home and abroad as the leading Irish poet of his generation and within Ireland as a controversial leader of the cultural nationalists seeking to recover (some would say invent) traditional materials for the creation of a modern Irish art and identity.

That process of self-fashioning followed the outlines of a perceptive comment with which Yeats began a retrospective essay composed in his mid-fifties called "If I Were Four-and-Twenty." There he wrote of his youth:

> *One day when I was twenty-three or twenty-four this sentence seemed to form in my head, without my willing it, much as sentences form when we are half-asleep: "Hammer your thoughts into unity." For days I could think of nothing else, and for years I tested all I did by that sentence. I had three interests: interest in a form of literature, in a form of philosophy, and a belief in nationality. None of these seemed to have anything to do with the other, but gradually my love of literature and my belief in nationality came together. Then for years I said to myself that these two had nothing to do with my form of philosophy, but that I had only to be sincere and to keep from constraining one by the other and they would become one interest.*

*Now all three are, I think, one, or rather all three are
a discrete expression of a single conviction. I think that
each has behind it my whole character and has gained
thereby a certain newness . . .*[2]

The manuscripts in the present volume display that development clearly. In the earliest ones, like the long narrative "Sir
Roland," Yeats appears primarily as a derivative poet of late
Victorian literary convention, often imitating still earlier eras.
Those from the later 1880s, like "The Outlaw's Bridal," show
the fusion of Yeats's literary interests with his political ones,
particularly in the Irish settings and subject matter that had
begun to pervade his work. Finally, the poems of the 1890s, like
"To a Sister of the Cross and the Rose," display the merging of
the already-joined literary and political interests with esoteric
philosophies of a theosophical or Rosicrucian sort. The "certain
newness" provided by both their subject matter and their technique reveals Yeats on the cusp of developing the "modern"
style that he would make famous.

While one may track that progress through Yeats's published
poetry as well, the manuscripts used for *Under the Moon* allow a
look behind the scenes, at what was going on in Yeats's poetic
workshop during this important period. Although these poems
are not known to have been published by Yeats, it is possible that
some of the more polished among them did appear in fugitive
publications of late nineteenth-century Ireland. For example,
had a printed text of "The Protestants' Leap" not been discovered recently in a fragmentary copy of *The Gael* (the magazine
of the Gaelic Athletic Association) from 1887, that poem would
have been part of the present edition.[3] Further, at least two more

of the lyrics included here got as far as being set in proof. But Yeats chose to leave the majority of the poems unpublished. As such, they stand in the same relation to his individually published poems that those poems do to his single volumes of verse, and that those single volumes do to the collected ones. At every stage, Yeats constructed a self by inclusion, exclusion, and revision out of a wide range of available materials. Reading the early stages of that process can both illuminate the beginning of a major poetic career and add insight into the greater achievements that were to follow.

"I am persuaded that our intellects at twenty contain all the truths we shall ever find, but as yet we do not know truths that belong to us from opinions caught up in casual irritation or momentary fantasy," confessed Yeats in his *Autobiographies*.[4] The poems published here dating from that period (roughly, the first two dozen) support that claim. Among the false starts and derivative echoes appear some of Yeats's characteristic themes, such as disappointed love in "A double moon or more ago" or "The Magpie," valorization of the outcast in "Behold the man" or "For clapping hands," loss of a golden age in "Pan," or the representation of vision in "The Old Grey Man" or "I sat upon a high gnarled root." At least as important as individual themes is their deployment in a pattern of opposites that Yeats would later call "antinomies" and would embed as basic contrasts throughout his work. "I spend my days correcting proofs," he wrote to his longtime confidante and former lover Olivia Shakespear in 1932 while revising the canon of his poetry for a collected edition. "I have just finished the first volume, all my lyric poetry, and am greatly astonished at myself. . . . I keep saying what man is this who . . . says the same thing in so many different ways. . . . The swordsman throughout repudiates the saint, but not without vacillation. Is that perhaps the sole theme —Usheen and Patrick . . . ?"⁵ Usheen (Oisin) and Patrick, the chief characters in *The Wanderings of Oisin,* represent such antinomies as active versus contemplative life, pagan versus Christian Ireland, and acceptance of the world versus transcendence of it. Those same contrasts, along with many others, appear in the poems here, as they do throughout Yeats's work.

Images and symbols that he would later make famous arise here, too, like the questers in "Sir Roland," the tower of "Tower wind-beaten grim," or the symbolic geography of fountains, dells, boats, and sun and moon that dot the poems. The bird imagery of several lyrics finds its most striking anticipation of the later work in the golden bird that adorns the cover of an album containing nine of the poems and that inevitably suggests the more famous golden bird of Yeats's two Byzantium poems. Not surprisingly, the forms of the early verse anticipate those used in several of Yeats's greatest achievements. The experimentation with sonnet structure in "Behold the man" or "The Veiled Voices" would lead to such great mature sonnets as "Leda and the Swan" or "Meru." Yeats's fondness for dialogue poems here runs the gamut from relatively simple interchanges in "The Magpie" and "A soul of the fountain" to the full-blown ones of "Love's Decay." He would later compose numerous major poems in dialogue, including "The Mask," "Ego Dominus Tuus," and "A Dialogue of Self and Soul." And the preference for eight-line units that underlies "A Prayer for My Daughter" or "The Municipal Gallery Re-visited" appears as early as "The Magpie" and "The Outlaw's Bridal."

Yeats composed with considerable difficulty, and even these

early poems show his lifelong concern over poetic craft. "Metrical composition is always very difficult to me, nothing is done upon the first day, not one rhyme is in its place; and when at last the rhymes begin to come, the first rough draft of a six-line stanza takes the whole day," he wrote while recollecting his early career in his autobiography. "At that time I had not formed a style, and sometimes a six-line stanza would take several days, and not seem finished even then."[6] The little lyric "Pan" exemplifies Yeats's care in composition. The version included here is based on the last of nine separate manuscript drafts, each with revisions, which yields a total of eighteen surviving stages of evolution for this one lyric alone. Particularly in early drafts, Yeats had difficulty with meter as well as form. "I had begun to write poetry in imitation of Shelley and of Edmund Spenser," he recalled in another section of the autobiography. "My lines but seldom scanned, for I could not understand the prosody in the books, although there were many lines that taken by themselves had music."[7] That problem shows itself even in the advanced drafts of some of the earliest poems in *Under the Moon*, though by the time of the last poems Yeats had discovered how to make his own music. Besides difficulties with form and meter, Yeats had problems with spelling as well. With weak vision throughout his life (he may have been mildly dyslexic), Yeats's misadventures with orthography can hearten those of us who suffer from similar problems. In the manuscript of one poem alone, "Sir Roland," a partial list of slips would include "rippened," "dreemer," "vessul," "fragence," "impasible," "fearce," and "insasiate." Not surprisingly in view of such difficulties, Yeats tended to hoard and recycle verse that he had brought to an advanced state with such trouble. He often used passages from unpublished poems as quarries for published work, and some of the early published poems originated in unpublished plays. That was true of sections of poems, too. For example, the lines in the present volume about Aeneas's "ships / Enamoured of the waves' impetuous lips" reemerge in Yeats's first major published work, *The Island of Statues.*[8]

With his literary interests well-established, Yeats was soon to join them with Irish nationalism. Up until 1885 his existence had oscillated among Dublin, where he was born and sometimes lived, London, where his father, the painter John Butler Yeats, had moved the family in search of commissions, and the west-country port of Sligo, where his mother's relatives lived. Unsure of his ability to pass the entrance examinations for the Anglo-Irish citadel of Trinity College Dublin, Yeats in 1884 had entered instead the Metropolitan School of Art. But his literary interests continued strong, taking a decisive turn when he met the exiled Irish patriot John O'Leary shortly after O'Leary's return to Ireland the following year. Yeats maintained consistently that the event had changed his art and his life. "It was through the old Fenian leader John O'Leary I found my theme," he recalled in the late essay "A General Introduction for My Work." "His long imprisonment, his longer banishment, his magnificent head, his scholarship, his pride, his integrity, all that aristocratic dream nourished amid little shops and little farms, had drawn around him a group of young men."[9] Yeats quickly became a member of that group, and eventually O'Leary's favorite disciple. O'Leary championed a fusion of literature and nationalism, and so did Yeats. For example, in *Letters to the New Island,* a collection of pieces written for American journals between 1888 and 1892, Yeats invoked his mentor as sanction for the principle that "there is no fine nationality without literature, and . . . there is no fine literature without nationality."[10]

Yeats's own poetry would henceforth feature Irish materials with increasing frequency. At first, these seemed to consist more of invoking Irish settings for not very Irish works, or writing picturesquely of faeries and folk. Yet from such unpromising beginnings would come great later works, such as "The Tower" or "In Memory of Major Robert Gregory." Among the poems in *Under the Moon* "The Outlaw's Bridal" offers a ready example of Yeats's early turn toward Irish subjects. The general situation of an outlaw chieftan and his lover fleeing pursuit, and contrast between life outside social conventions and inside them, fits much of Yeats's earlier reading and composition, such as "Hushed in the vale of Dagestan." Yet the subtitle "Ireland 16—" immediately locates the narrative in Ireland, perhaps particularly during the brutal Cromwellian period in which Yeats also set the recently rediscovered "The Protestants' Leap." The outlaw's claim to have named his horse after "great Brian" recalls Brian Boru, the famous medieval high king of Ireland. The persistent though generalized references to the mountains and shores of the West evoke both the resistant heartland of Gaelic Ireland and the region from Clare and Galway to Connemara and Sligo that Yeats would later commemorate more specifically. And the allusion to "my land's long battle" inevitably suggests Ireland's long struggle against English domination, which in "Under Ben Bulben" Yeats would later term "seven heroic centuries." Yet as a whole the poem seems more a transference of derivative literary models to an Irish environment than a convincing representation of some form of Irishness. What the poem catches is not Yeats's mature fusion of nationality and literature, but rather the pivotal moment when he began to move in that direction. The slightly later "The Watch-Fire" shows him a step further down that road, in a nationalist ballad evocative of Thomas Davis's "Young Ireland" tradition.

Besides literature and Irish nationalism, the third interest that Yeats identified in "If I Were Four-and-Twenty" was esoteric philosophy. The year he met O'Leary, 1885, also marked his first formal involvement with occult societies, in this case the Dublin Hermetic Society, which he helped to found. There Yeats, his friend Charles Johnston, and others would discuss the "esoteric Buddhism" of A. P. Sinnett, the theosophy of Mohini Chatterjee and Madame Blavatsky, and other occult doctrines. The sympathetic though skeptical Yeats hoped to find in such doctrines an alternative to scientific materialism and a connection to a spiritual world behind the physical one. He also found in them liberation from his father's more rationalist and utilitarian outlook: "It was only when I began to study psychical research and mystical philosophy that I broke away from my father's influence," recalled Yeats.[11] That study of psychical research and mystical philosophy continued with Yeats's joining the Esoteric Section of the London Theosophical Society in 1888, where he particularly pursued occult phenomena along with the society's broader devotion to Indian philosophy and mystic doctrine. Partly because of his skepticism, Yeats was asked to resign two years later, but by then he had already joined the Hermetic Order of the Golden Dawn, a group more explicitly devoted to Rosicrucian lore.

Although even in the mid-1880s Yeats wrote of magicians and sorcerers (particularly female ones, like the title character in *Mosada* or the Enchantress in *The Island of Statues*), explicit esoteric doctrine joined with his literary and national interests most markedly for the first time in the poems of the early 1890s. Several lyrics in the current collection exemplify that fusion, perhaps best of all "To a Sister of the Cross and the Rose." Its very title suggests Rosicrucian tradition, a bundle of mystical and magical doctrine deriving from Father Christian Rosenkreuz (or Rosicross) and highlighted by the title *The Rosy Cross—Lyrics* that Yeats gave to the decorated manuscript collection from which it comes. In 1899 Yeats would for the first time use a design featuring rose and cross for the revised edition of his collected *Poems,* originally published in 1895 and his best-known book for the next quarter-century. The Rose, too, suggested a range of additional meanings played on in *The Rose* section of the collected poems, a range that included Irish nationalist significance along with the philosophic or esoteric meaning. The image also included literary application, for in his 1895 essay on "The Body of Father Christian Rosencrux" Yeats identified the preserved body of Rosencrux with "the imagination," which had "been laid in a great tomb of criticism" but was currently on the verge of renewal.[12] Thus, the lyric, characteristically written in an eight-line stanza, itself blends Yeats's interests in literary, national, and esoteric revivals, with the morning bugles (endearingly misspelled "buggles") of the last line suggesting a renewal on all three levels:

> *No daughter of the Iron Times,*
> *　The Holy Future summons you;*
> *　Its voice is in the falling dew*
> *In quiet star light, in these rhymes,*
> *In this sad heart consuming slow—*

Cast all good common hopes away,
For I have seen the enchanted day
And heard the morning bugles blow.

August
1891

The lyric also exemplifies a fourth level to add to the other three, the erotic. Yeats would become one of the great love poets in the language, and the poems here from the 1890s demarcate the change from the derivative and rather unconvincing amorous verse of the 1880s to the more powerful and passionate later work. That transformation coincided with his famous passion for Maud Gonne, the beautiful and charismatic nationalist leader whom he met in 1889 and who became for many years the center of his emotional life. "I had never thought to see in a living woman so great beauty," he wrote. "It belonged to famous pictures, to poetry, to some legendary past."[13] Often the resultant poetry stayed at a general if intense romantic level, but sometimes it pertained more directly to Gonne. The title "To a Sister of the Cross and the Rose," for example, glances at Gonne's forthcoming initiation as a "soror" or sister of the Order of the Golden Dawn, while the poet's "sad heart" of line 5 reflects a frequent pose of Yeats's poetic speakers during his long-frustrated courtship of Gonne.

Two other poems feature intimate aspects of the Yeats-Gonne relationship and may have been suppressed for just that reason. "A Dream of a Life Before This One" recalls a dream that Gonne confided to Yeats in which "she and I had been brother and sister somewhere on the edge of the Arabian desert, and sold together into slavery."[14] Characteristically, the experience moved Yeats to another of his fruitless proposals of marriage to Gonne. More sensationally, "On a Child's Death" commemorates the death by meningitis of one-year-old Georges, the illegitimate child whom Gonne had with the French political journalist Lucien Millevoye. The poem itself is dated September 5, 1893, two years after the death of the child, by which time Yeats had learned more of the true circumstances of Georges's birth than he had known originally. The poem itself also offers a vignette of Gonne amidst part of the menagerie of animals with which she liked to surround herself.

Simply to transfer some of the unpublished poems of the 1890s from their manuscript sources to the present printed book without calling attention to their original context would obscure important features. Modern textual theorists increasingly distinguish between the "linguistic code" of a work (its words) and its "bibliographic code" (all aspects of its physical incarnation). The bibliographic code of the last eight poems in the present volume includes manuscript books of varying elaborateness in design and arrangement that Yeats constructed in the early 1890s, together with other sources. "To a Sister," "The Pathway," and "He who bids," for example, appeared successively as three of the six poems composing *The Rosy Cross—Lyrics,* a manuscript album assembled by Yeats in late 1891. The same three, together with an earlier version of "A Dream of a Life Before This One," also appear in an overlapping manuscript collection, the even more elaborate *Flame of the Spirit,* which Yeats presented to Maud Gonne as a love token in October 1891. Yeats was one of the most architectonic of lyric poets, and those poems—like his others—profit from being studied in their original sequence and arrangement. Further, the construction of the manuscript books themselves gestures toward a more courtly time preceding industrial book production, a gesture not only of nostalgia for an epoch thought to be more hospitable to what Yeats elsewhere called "the old high way of love" but also of resistance to those social and economic aspects of modern society which Yeats most distrusted. The bibliographic codes enable him to play both courtly lover to Gonne and critic of contemporary society at the same time.[15]

The title of the present volume itself gestures toward a lost bibliographic code. *Under the Moon* was the title that Yeats originally intended for the major gathering of his early work eventually published as *Poems* in 1895. In addition to the normal literary and philosophical connotations of chance and change, Yeats intended a supplementary, Irish meaning. A publisher's paragraph probably based on one supplied by Yeats himself for a publicity release read in part: "Old writers were of opinion that the moon governed by her influence peasants, sailors, fishermen, and all obscure persons; and as the symbols of Mr. Yeats's poetry are taken almost wholly from the tradition and manners of the Connaught peasantry, he has selected the title 'Under the Moon' for his forthcoming book."[16] The title itself, then, reflects Yeats's desire expressed in the essay "If I Were Four-and-Twenty" to fuse literary, philosophic, and national interests—to hammer his thoughts into unity. *Under the Moon* gives us a new glimpse of the workshop where that was done.

NOTES TO INTRODUCTION

1. While a few of the poems have been reproduced in specialized monographs or scholarly journals, over two dozen appear here in reading texts for the first time. The versions in the present volume are edited clear texts. For literal transcriptions of the various drafts, and detailed information about the manuscripts, see my recent *W. B. Yeats, The Early Poetry, Vol. II: "The Wanderings of Oisin" and Other Early Poems to 1895—Manuscript Materials* (Ithaca and London: Cornell University Press, 1994).

2. *Explorations* (New York: Macmillan, 1963), p. 263.

3. See *The Poems* (revised), ed. Richard J. Finneran (New York: Macmillan, 1989), p. 512. The published form of "The Protestants' Leap" was recovered by John S. Kelly, who discusses it in his perceptive "Aesthete among the Athletes: Yeats's Contributions to *The Gael*," in *Yeats: An Annual*

of Critical and Textual Studies, ed. Richard J. Finneran, vol. II (Ithaca: Cornell University Press, 1984), pp. 75–143.

4. W. B Yeats, *Autobiographies* (London: Macmillan, 1966), p. 189.

5. *Letters,* ed. Allan Wade (New York: Macmillan, 1955), p. 798.

6. Yeats, *Autobiographies,* p. 202.

7. Yeats, *Autobiographies,* p. 67.

8. *The Poems,* p. 481.

9. *Essays and Introductions* (New York: Macmillan, 1961), p. 510.

10. *Letters to the New Island,* ed. George Bornstein and Hugh Witemeyer (New York: Macmillan, 1989), p. 12.

11. Yeats, *Autobiographies,* p. 89.

12. *Essays and Introductions,* p. 196.

13. *Memoirs,* ed. Denis Donoghue (London: Macmillan, 1972), p. 40.

14. *Memoirs,* p. 46.

15. For fuller description of the bibliographic codes and of the manuscript albums see *W. B. Yeats: The Early Poetry, Volume II* and also the notes to the present volume.

16. *Collected Letters of W. B. Yeats,* vol. I, ed. John S. Kelly and Eric Domville (Oxford: Oxford University Press, 1986), p. 411.

NOTE ON THE TEXTS

The present edition presents reading texts of thirty-eight un-published early poems by W. B. Yeats. The interested reader will find diplomatic (verbatim) transcriptions of the manuscripts, including revisions, in my *W. B. Yeats: The Early Poetry, Volume II,* recently published in the Cornell Yeats series (Ithaca and London: Cornell University Press). Because the Cornell edition represented the manuscripts themselves as literally as possible for scholars, I have here tried instead to present the texts in easily readable form for a broader audience. While opting for conservative policies that intervene in the text only minimally, I have used the following guidelines for presenting works written in Yeats's often difficult handwriting and sometimes wayward orthography and punctuation:

1. *Spelling, capitalization, and spacing have been standardized.*
2. *Abbreviations have been expanded.*

3. *Yeats usually composed with very little or sometimes even no punctuation. Here, punctuation has been added sparingly in the interest of clarifying the sense in those cases where the syntax seemed to dictate a particular choice, but the introduction of copious new punctuation that would close off equally likely alternatives has been avoided.*

4. *Where Yeats supplied titles, those have been adopted. Where he did not, I have with two exceptions followed the customary practice of adopting the first line as title. The two exceptions are the narrative poem "Sir Roland" and the dramatic scene "Cyprian," for which adopting the name of the principal character as title seemed a more useful mnemonic device.*

5. *Where Yeats's difficult handwriting allowed for more than one reading, I have chosen the one that appeared more likely. In the few cases where a word remains illegible, it is indicated by a question mark within square brackets.*

6. *Rather than adopting an arbitrary numerical grid, I have provided line numbering adapted to stanza form or to syntax where feasible.*

7. *In the Notes at the end of the volume, a headnote to each poem offers brief information about such subjects as the manuscript's location, its time of composition (where known), form or theme, and relation to Yeats's other work. Notes keyed to individual lines identify specific allusions or problems there.*

Readers curious about the exact manuscript evidence will find physical descriptions of the manuscripts together with their literal transcriptions in *W. B. Yeats: The Early Poetry, Volume II*. All of the manuscripts of the twenty-nine "Poems of the 1880s" are in the National Library of Ireland, except for "Wherever in the wastes," which is in the Huntington Library. With the exception of a sheet of galley proof in the collection of Anne Butler Yeats, a version of another poem in canceled proof at Yale University, and a version of a third at Emory University, the manuscripts for the nine "Poems of the 1890s" are in three manuscript notebooks: one entitled "The Rosy Cross. Lyrics," in the National Library of Ireland, one entitled "Flame of the Spirit," sold at auction at Sotheby's in July 1987 and now reportedly in a private Irish collection, and a white vellum album that I consulted when it was in the collection of Michael Butler Yeats and that recently has been transferred to the collection of Boston College. Virtually all manuscripts in the collection of the National Library of Ireland or of Michael Butler Yeats are also accessible on microform at the Department of Special Collections of the library of the State University of New York at Stony Brook.

The dedication to this volume is meant to acknowledge the exemplary care and generosity with which Anne, Michael, and Gráinne Yeats have handled their responsibilities toward W. B. Yeats's manuscripts and other materials, even while pursuing their own distinguished careers. I am grateful as well to Richard J. Finneran for his scholarly advice and for reading an advanced version of the present book. I should also like to thank Jonathan Allison, Richard Badenhausen, Conrad Balliet, Angela Bourke, Mary FitzGerald, Roy Foster, Warwick Gould, George Mills Harper, Miranda Hickman, David Holdeman, Carolyn Holdsworth, John Hollander, Marjorie Howes, Heather Bryant Jordan, John Kelly, Greg Kucich, the late F. S. L. Lyons, Edward O'Shea, the late Thomas Parkinson, Stephen Parrish, Ronald Schuchard, Mary Helen Thuente, and Robert Weisbuch. The staffs of the National Library of Ireland, the Huntington Library, the Woodruff Library at Emory University, the Beinecke Library at Yale University, and the Melville Memorial Library at the State University of New York at Stony Brook provided both cooperation and assistance.

POEMS

OF

THE

1880s

1. A flower has blossomed

A flower has blossomed, the world heart core,
The petals and leaves were a moon white flame.
A gathered the flower, the colourless lore
The abundant measure of fate and fame.
Many men gather and few may use
The sacred oil and the sacred cruse.

2. *A double moon or more ago*

A double moon or more ago
    I writ you a long letter, lady,
    It went astray or vexed you, maybe,
And I would know now yes or no.

Then dying Summer on his throne
    Faded in hushed and quiet singing
    Now Winter's arrow's winging, winging,
And Autumn's yellow leaves are flown.   8

Ah we poor poets in our pride
    Tread the bare song road all our summer,
    To wake on lips of some new comer
"A poor man lived here once and died."

How could we trudge on mile by mile
    If from red lips like quicken berry,
    At some odd times to make us merry,
Came nowise half of half a smile?   16

And surely therefore would I know
    What manner fared my letter, lady,
    It went astray or vexed you maybe
A double moon or more ago.

3. *Behold the man*

Behold the man—Behold his brow of care,
   He sought to stay the living and the dead
   That pass'd like shadows o'er an osier bed
On which from her high cloud-embosomed lair
The sick moon peers—He plucked them by the hair
   And bade them stay. They smiled and passing led
   Their ancient way—the living and the dead—
As o'er the sea from love-sick Dido's stair   8
   Passed long ago the wanderer's white sailed ships
   Enamoured of the waves' impetuous lips.
He sighing rose and took his way at length
   In rage inhuman—He who sought for more
   Than all the nations with their famous lore
Of love—alone a sad forsaken strength.

WBY
March 8th 1884

4. Sir Roland

1.

When to its end o'er-ripened July nears
One lurid eve befell mine history—
No rime empassioned of envenomed years
Or the embattled earth—a song should be
A painted and be-pictured argosy,
And as a crew to guide her wandering days
Sad love and change yea those that sisters be
For they upon each other's eyes do gaze
And they do whisper in each other's ears always.   9

2.

As gently down the apple blossom dropped
As is the muffled tread of misery,
The creepers that no envious sickle cropt
With flowers bemisted every plumy tree
In Lethe's valley by the silent sea,
And then at times from out the wood advances
A shadowy thing and where the billows flee
Along the sand and 'mong their foamy glances
A moment to and fro the elfin shadow dances.   18

3.

Upon the hem of the unfruitful sand
An old man passed with visage worn and wan
And time had seamed his brow with many a band,
A Templar cross of red was sewn upon
His shoulders thin, his eyes but dimly shone
And he at times at that thing or at this
Of memory would smile, but had when done
A pilgrim's face—O lonely thy path is
The way. His comrades are mainly 'mong the dead I wis.   27

4.

He drew anigh to where upon the south
Clothed in a wood of hazel and of lime
'Mong goblin fruitage gazed the haunted valley's mouth.
Weak voicéd he began an ancient rime—
The long waves were a chorus with their chime—
A song forlorn about a lady fair
Who in the old forgotten barbarous time
In iron Norway loved a dead corsair
And till she faded would across the dim seas stare.   36

[5.

Sir Roland passed in singing that old stave
Within the mouth of Lethe's vale profound
That gazed across the ever labouring wave,
And there there seeméd breathing from the ground
In all the dim and dolorous vale around
Some soul forlorn of old unhappy love
And from the waves now veiled with trees a sound
Of sighs and from the vale and trees thereof
And from the fruited creepers hanging from above.]   45

6.

And now within the valley's mouth he came
Upon his ears the sun by night appalled
Sank slowly seaward rolled in horded flame;
The fakéd fire within the valley crawled
Along the giant fruits the owlets called
A ghastly ever-growing company
From where the steep some long dead man had walled,
Soon all things else but these things sleeping be,
The owls that hoot round cliff and wall and crumbling tree.   54

[6.

Anigh the valley's head a fountain sprang
Nearby a twisted fruit tree's shadow dappled
By bounteous eve begilded while it sang—
Beneath the trees when autumn comes, o'er-appled
Now flower-pale—upon the shadow dappled
A huge knight lay whose calm eyes softly shed
A far-off gaze as of some ghost unchapelled
Of one who once in immemorial ages bled
Yea as the far-off gaze of one for ages dead.   63

7.

So far the joys and sorrows of the world
Had fled from him who lay where eve's red flake
Of flame dancéd upon the fountain curled,
And old he was, he to Sir Roland spake:
"Old man, whence comest thou for what deeds
Thus heavy armed, for gleamings clear of plated mail
From 'mong the crimson of thy vestments break?
O knight, for thou art such, what rumoured tale
Of high emprizes leads thee unto Lethe's vale?"]   72

8.

Then Roland spake: "Old knight, drawn unto thee
I come upon no quest of high renown,
Of late I rode upon a far journey
But fain to ease mine horse I lighted down
Thinking to go afoot along the brown
Sea sand for he was weary with the way,
But sudden from a bursting billow's crown
A sea snake glided and in wild dismay
My good horse fled, wherefore within the valley grey   81

9.

I seek thy help, o thou whom Mary keep."
Then rose the dreamer and while a drooping bough
Of apple blossom light as fairy sleep
Snowed o'er with crimson all the dreamer's brow,
And through the silence of the valley now
Passed on these twain. The history of the vale
Sir Roland longed for eagerly I trow
Yet would not ask—but soon unbade this tale
The clear-browed dreamer told within the hollow dale.   90

10.

"I ruled of yore a land where warless castles
Lay by their fields of grain and cattle folds
—A feastful land—I ruled o'er joyous vassals
Who gathered often in my castle hold
Where sea tales on the winter eves were told
By some swart rover who with his long vessels
Measured the seas for merchandize or gold
Where some spice isle upon the ocean nestles
Or wind with polar water in the darkness wrestles.   99

11.

I was most blest fore all mine were, the coy
And wild lark liberty who hath her broods
'Mong barren hills and the swift blind eagle joy—
And love who seeks alone dear solitudes
To muse on her high kinsman grief—the woods
And water saw the boundaries of my lands
And knew them wide—yet by the fleecy floods
All these I did renounce when homeward bands
Of hunters left me lingering 'lone upon the sands.   108

[*12*.

Upon the surf-besiegéd shore I stood,
I stood and gazed upon the leaping wave.
The funeral pyre of day was red as blood,
The white maned horses of the sea did rave
Where the fire did descend himself to lave
Forgetful of their ancient flood. Within
And then I saw a plunging vessel drave
Forth from the flame yea from the flame and din
And soon her keel the surf-besiegéd shore did win.]   117

13.

And from her came a man like those of story
A dateless weariness was in his eyes
Unhuman sorrow and unhuman glory—
A raven darkest minion of the skies
Before him flew, and still before him flies,
And he anigh me drew and from a lyre
Within his [?   ] hands I heard arise
Sweet song but on my soul there came a fire
That never shall till comes the end of days expire.   126

14.

He sang of Ingiborg the fair dead maid
Whose feet a-roving are in harvest plain
Land of the Asphodels that never fade
O land beyond the springs of the swift rain.
He sang of how afar beyond the main
In vine-hung vales where summer hath her home
She will at times descend when evenings pale,
Then ceased the song—I gazed, and saw the foam
Smoking along the waves and heard their voices moan.   135

15.

But no black vessel lay among the surf
And no man with a raven by me was
Nor by the neighbouring vale whose plumy turf
Was heavy with the sheep-delighting grass
Nor by the wood-hung river did he pace.
Then musing I strode on mine homeward way;
Above the castle in a drowsy mass
The banner hung. The bees from toil of day
Were resting in their hives below the walls' old grey.   144

16.

And sudden round me did I summon them,
My dark sea-nurtured people every one,
And chose a stalwart crew of firm-souled men
And manned a vessel and when all was done
Forth from the shadow of the shore sailed on
From 'mong the mourning people, on we sailed
Till of the noise of the land were none
And last till fragrance of the harvest failed,
The throbbing stars were o'er us and the sea fowl hailed   153

17.

From wave to wave each other 'mong the foam,
And on we sailed by land the seas enfold
And shores where ceaseless summer hath her home
And where the vine is, still the live sea rolled
And the bell-tongued billows tolled and tolled and tolled
Around a fleeting ship, and man by man
My sea-worn sailors died and neath the mold
Of far-off isles were laid where their lives' span
Of wide world wandering to a lonely finish ran.   162

18.

Now here I dwelt upon the world's wide face
Those never more to be consoléd dwell
Here Joy and Sorrow have no dwelling place
Such as are echoes in some wave-worn shell
Mere dream-winged sounds that can no story tell,
My years shall flow in final pace I ween
Till I shall leave in silence this lone dell
And live within the wandering isle serene
With fair-haired Ingiborg the dead Norwegian queen."   171

19.

He ceased—the echoes of the hollow vale
Died slowly fondling the well-loved sound
Of that dear name through all the dinful dale
The flowers that among the branches wound
Seemed singing o'er the dim becharméd ground
With little voices sweet and numerous
"With joy as deep we on our petals bound
When thy dear name descending dwells with us
As when the bees are on our petals luminous."   180

20.

As though in shadow of a willow tree
Drowsed Cupid weary grown of love and scorn
Till some name famous in his psaltery
Came dreaming on the sleeping ear out-worn,
And he went forth with torch and bow upborn
So swiftly in the windless valley there
The great fruits woke as in the song of morn
All swinging swinging swinging in the air
And in each gleamed a goblin fire wild and rare.   189

21.

They stood—the valley lilies those that listen
Forever with their ears upon the ground
Did round their feet along the pathway glisten.
Spake Roland, "Surely thou art he the sound
Of whose great name has gone the wide world round,
Olaf the hero Dane." "Yea I am he,"
The other spake. Now in a wood profound
The twain had come to where did Roland see
Among this dimness rise a cliff impassable.   198

2 1[a].

And all the voiceful legions of the land
Within the moonless windless night were still,
All slept I think—all save alone the falling sand
Of change who wrings from love her tokens ill
All else—Nay nay I wish each mountain rill
Was not unmindful of its weeping cry.
Impassable the cliff wall seemed until
They came the wood engirdled base anigh,
And then appeared a stairway on its surface high.   207

2 2.

Along the stair to where the cliff uprises
High as the roving kestrel sails they passed—
High as the kestrel whose fierce soul surmises
And dreams of quarry musing in the breast
That drives him ever onward fast and fast—
A cave they found anear the cliff wall's head—
The stars their brethren were—The earth was past,
Unto the listening stars the cavern shed
A muffled tune of hidden streams uncomforted,   216

23.

'Twas there the hermit knight Sir Olaf bode.
On either side a black stone figure bore
Upon his shoulders wide the ponderous lode
Of that wide dome which hung the cavern o'er
Down through a chasm in the riven floor
Belching above a stream did shrieking go,
One crouching statue at the waters hoar
Pointed for ever with his arm, as though
He numbered all the drops of water in their flow.   225

24.

The other's eyes were fixéd on the sky
The sleepless baleful eyeballs dark as night
He watched how rose and set continually
How ebbed and flowed the stars and planets bright
Mirrored upon his eye in wandering light
The stars a thousand ages rose and set   231

. . . .

27.

The weeping wind seemed ever singingly
Unto the vale that heard insatiate
To whisper some forlorn old history
Of some once fair now star bebaffled fate.
At last these words did grow articulate:
"Sansloy my name is, joy I ever seek,
O surely she doth somewhere hidden wait
By mere or mountain or by shady creek—
Hath thou seen joy?" and dying then the voice grew weak   240

28.

And ceased. The swift-tongued colloquist
The lonely sea sang forth these words anon:
"O vale, o shore my waves have often kissed,
Knowest thou me? Each wave-worn skeleton
Knows well my name Sansfoy, and ever on
Reaching the world for joy I rush and rush.
Tell me, o thou whose days in silence run,
Dost thou hold her from me, o valley lush?"
Then sudden fell upon the land a bodeful hush   249

29.

Till in the midmost of the elfin dale
Began a honeyed voice with veiled singing,
Then loud and swift till all the eager vale
By cliff and wood and reedy pool was ringing.
O spirit of the valley, song-soul flinging
Thy voice of tears upon the shrinking earth,
O nightingale most surely thou wert bringing
This answer in thy song: "O sea wave curled
O moth-like wings of wind, o wind with wings enfurled   258

30.

And wherefore question me thou sea and wind?
To muse on sorrow is my days' employ,
Twain whom in your searching no bands bind
Ye know not that I am named Sansjoy
The self-same as the long dead paynim boy
Yet this alone of all things do I know
That nothing's holy saving only joy"—
Died the song-soul's singing down below
And from the forms of stone there came an echo low.   267

END

5. Sansloy—Sansfoy—Sansjoy

'Tis of a vision heard and seen
   In a garden by the sea
On a day of gracious mien
   Once when o'er a lily spotted
   Broken all and pale and blotted
   O'er the lawn with daisies dotted
Came the wind along the green.   7

Cried the ever-roving wind,
   "Sansloy my name is—joy I seek,
Never chains my way shall bind."
   Cried the wave, "Full many a one
   Now a wave-worn skeleton
   Knew my name, Sansfoy, and on
Seeking joy I ever wind."   14

Sighed the lily, "White as snow
   Once my curving petals were,
Now drooping on my stem alow,
   And my name it is Sansjoy
   Selfsame as the paynim boy—
   Nothing's holy saving joy
This much only do I know."   21

                           Sept.

6. *The Priest of Pan*

If the melancholy music of the spheres
Ever be perplexing to his mortal ears,
He flies unto the mountain
And sitting by some fountain
That in a beam of coolness from a mossy rock
Plunges in a pool all bubbling with its shock,
There he hears in the sound of the water falling
The sweet-tongued oriads to each other calling   8
Secrets that for years
Have escaped his ears.

7. The Magpie

Over the heath has the magpie flown
  Over the hazel cover,
Ah why will a magpie live alone
  He waits for the lady and lover.
"What may be the sadness that ends your smile?"
  She said, "My peace is o'er, love"
"I am going afar for so brief a while"
  She said, "We must no more, love."   8

They stood for the swish of the mower's blade
  As they went round the meadow,
And under him as he sang and swayed
  Moved his meridian shadow.
"The ruddy young reaper he sings be glad
  In the sphere of the earth is no flaw, love."
She said, "He is singing all lives grown sad
  He knows no other law, love."   16

The grass and the sedge and the little reed wren
  A sociable world were talking
And the water was saying enough for ten
  As they by the stream went walking.
"The grass and the sedge and the little reed wren
  Are saying it low and high, love,
There's a feast in the forest and mirth in the fen."
  She said, "Ah how they sigh, love."   24

He flew by the meadow and flew by the brake
  She saw him over the flag fly
Down by the marsh, with his tail a-shake
  Alone with himself the magpie.
"What may be the sadness that ends your smile?"
  She said, "My peace is o'er, love."
Ah who with folly from love beguiled
  She said, "We must no more, love."   32

8. 'Mong meadows of sweet grain

'Mong meadows of sweet grain and musing kine
Wanders my little rivulet. I like
Her more than those mad singers who passed by,
And following her shaded shores I'll rest
Where she within the cherry orchard sings
Forever in the bulrush beds about
Herself and to herself, sweet egotist.

9. *I heard a rose on the brim*

I heard a rose on the brim
Of the moss in the wood-ways dim
   On a rock's rim,
Where prating the black birds meet
   Where the paw of the squirrel rushes,
   Sing to the soft wind's gushes
A song that was giddy and sweet.   7

"Dear wind I long to rest
Upon thy song-heaved breast,
   Wind of the west."
I saw the fingers close
   Of the wind on the ruined glow,
   I saw scattered petals a-blow.
Ah rose, poor love-sick rose.   14

10. Hushed in the vale of Dagestan

1.

Hushed in the vale of Dagestan
I lay alone pierced through with lead,
Out of a smoky wound blood ran
And curled beneath my heavy head.

2.

The cliffs clung near in yellow bands,
The sunlight burnt their horned steeps
And burnt me where among the sands
I slept the heedless sleep of sleeps.   8

3.

And as I lay I dreamt a dream
Of feasting in my native vale
And young wives gathering in the gleam
To tell of me a lisping tale.

4.

And one was there in sadness swathed
She was not of the lispering round,
But with her hands before her bathed
Her soul in revery profound.   16

5.

Far off there in hollow Dagestan
She saw a well-known corpse abide,
And drip on drip the black blood ran
Down from the gaping tattered side.

11. For clapping hands

For clapping hands of all men's love
Oh poet still the fire of longing,
They pass and where you live above
In golden freedom there come thronging
The foolish wisemen with their words.
Live thou in calmness though cold herds
Shall fling ephemeral laughter round
Thy throne where wrapt in dreams profound   8
There forms the fruitage of thy days,
Inborn is its own melodious praise.
Ye censorious man thou art
In thou thyself the judge of judges,
Hath e'r contentment, let thy heart
Bid the mad mob that neath thee trudges
If thou hast known contentment mock
Thy labour, aye, and bid them rock   16
The altar from its place and spit,
Hid where the sacred fire was lit
With offices of reverend hands,
Aye aye, and where the sacred tripod stands.

1 2. An Old and Solitary One

They say I'm proud and solitary, yes proud,
Because my love and hate abideth ever
A changeless thing among the changing crowd
Until the sleep, an high soul changes never.

This crowd that mock at me, their love and hate
Rove through the world and find no lasting home,
Two spectral things that beg at many a gate
O they are lighter than the windy foam.   8

Full often have I loved in olden days
But those I loved their hot hearts changéd ever
To coldness some and some to hate—always
I am the same, an high soul changes never.

And often when I loved I fain would hate
And when I hated find for love an home,
But have not changed though waxing old of late
But they are lighter than the windy foam.   16

And therefore I am proud and sad forever
Until the sleep, an high soul changes never;
The crowd, their love and hate hath never home,
O they are lighter than the windy foam.

13. *The Veiled Voices and the Questions of the Dark*

As me upon my way the tram car whirled
On through the night, thus did I moralize:
Yon Pharisee who dreams how goes the world
And how it runs awry, what secret lies
Within his lonely heart? And yonder weak
Far burst of laughter falling on mine ears
Shrill voiced—The gaudy vessel of old tears
What is its tale?

              Yon wretch of whom none speak,   8
Hoarder of shame when she has lost the sun
And her poor tragedy is o'er and done
And sealed and finished her unsummered days,
What gossip (surely even she has one)
Grown moody for a little while will shun
The old companions, the well trodden ways?

14. *A soul of the fountain*

A soul of the fountain spake me a word:
"Tell me the word of thy spirit's pleasure
For ever my deeds in Abeysherd
Laughter and dust to fashion of treasure."
I gave to the spirit an answering word:
"Out of an ancient book I've heard   6

'Be bold' the sage of old hath said,
'Be bold, be bold, and bold be ever more
And yet be not too bold,' thus have I read
Out of some famous book of ancient lore,
This is the word of my spirit's pleasure
Deep in its heart there is secret treasure."   12

I cast my line in the nethermost deep
Sounding the land where the fishes are
In the land of the visionary soul of sleep
Out of the ship of Azolar,
And I heard the laughs of scaly things
And the gleam and the flash of scaly rings.   18

I sought the ore in a rocky mount
And often I sundered the rock to find
If hollowed it were of bubbling fount,
And then I smote on the marbley rind,
Of late I smote on the mountain about
And as did the sea then answered the land: 24

"Far and near my hand takes measure
And out of the silver and gold comes earth
And out of the dust comes plenteous treasure,
Diaphanous gleam of Edenic birth."
O late I stood on the mountain's ground,
And as did the sea then answered the ground.   30

15. Cyprian

Cyprian—
I live in this lake-girt tropic island
Never a human eye has seen it
Never a boat has touched its magic strand.
Long centuries ago I pitied man
And passed o'er the world a spirit of unrest
And rebellion 'gainst the race of sleeping gods,
But men were mad and thought that they were blest
Misery was but a toll for living   8
That Olympian Zeus was good and slept
That the devil of the robber nation
Was good though they for all ages wept.
Yet though I am cursed with immortality
I was molden with a human nature.
With the centuries old age came on me
And weary of flying from the wrath of nations
I long since crossed the mountains   16
Seeking some peace from the world's throbbing
And sought out a little plaining fountain
Blaming because no nymph had decked his valley.
And then I spoke a word to it, a word of might,
And it heard the oreads' language
It spread a lake of glittering light.
Then once more I spoke that tongue
And there rose a stately island   24
Bright with the radiance of its flowers
And I stood upon its dry stream.

16. My song thou knowest

My song thou knowest of a dreaming castle—
    The pensive walls are like a woven net
    For cunning corbeils are in carving set
Of fair flowers in a wreathed tassel—
    From old world pages have they singing met.

17. The world is but a strange romance

The world is but a strange romance
The end is lost by woeful chance.
I am but a Troubador
Scholar in the woodlands' lore
Scholar in the songs of birds
And the flowers' whispered words
And the chimes the hairbells ring
As their heads in the breezes swing.   8

18. *The Old Grey Man*

Sudden as I sat in a wood
An old grey man before me stood
And his eyes were burning with molten fire
And he touched the notes of a silver lyre.
It was like the voice of spring
As to it he thus did sing:
 "Many have sung of maiden fair
 Many have sung of golden hair   8
 Many have sung of eyes of blue,
 I sing of high born maiden too.
 Of maidens all she is the peerless
 O no mortal has a face so sweet
 Around each man's heart she has wrapt a tress
 Of the blazing hair that rolls to her feet.
 Her voice is the treacherous echo
 And her eyes are those flames of yellow 16
 That play with flick'ring light
 Above the marsh at night."
He ceased. I held a wild thorn rose,
I looked up—the grey man was gone,
But the long haired scald
What was he called?
Was he the mind of the rose?
——————— Who knows?   24
I heard the caw of a distant rook
And the gurgle of a far off brook.

19. The Dell

All the bees that in this country dwell
Flying hither to this favoured dell
Rob the honey from the blue hairbell
Or fall victim to the chase
Of some geni of the place
Who hid deep within the purple rim
With tight drawn bow awaiteth him.
He will have no other powers   8
Among his own beloved flowers,
For merry fairies love to sip
Sweet nectar from the flower's lip.

20. *Inscription for a Christmas Card*

In this ruddy time of holly
This my greeting unto thee
By paths of crimson flowers
Untasted by the honey bee
By his solitary bowers.
Hand in hand may old time call thee
Where the wood spirits stately race
Flits ever on before thy face.   8
The great world for gold is mad
Content be thou that thou art glad
For riches go upon no quest:
Peace and solitude is best.
Hear ye not the tumbling waters
Rolling from the haunted hills,
Hear ye not the mountain's daughters
Laughing in a thousand rills,   16
Does not the shouting spring
Come on the swallow's wing?
Let there be all thy wealth.

21. *Tower wind-beaten grim*

1.

Tower wind-beaten grim
  The warmth of the ivy
  Has shrunken from thee,
It saw the mocking grin

2.

Of the ghosts on thy battlement,
  The ghosts of thy thousand years,
  And shaken with creeping fears
The green tendrils back from you bent.   8

3.

Once there rested a scholarly owl
  Hooting in a grey stone nook,
  Midnight chimed. The tower shook.
He heard the spirits frolic and howl.

4.

The owl flew far through the night
  And much to himself did moan,
  At last he fell like a stone
He was quite dead of fright.   16

5.

Scatter-brained as a common fowl
  Thus died this learned bird
  Because he simply heard
An anti-philosophic howl.

22. *Sunrise*

The young leaves spring, the cattle low,
The torrents in the valley go
On thirsting for the ocean's flow,
     Loud they rejoice
     Hearing his voice.
Reddning is the mountain's comb,
Voices as of elf or gnome
Through the twisted valleys roam
     And gently croon
     That ancient rune,   10
At the touch of Proserpine
Of the loom among the pine
Swept from every golden line
     How it sweeps
     Up the steeps,
Round each heather bell it floats
While merle and throstle gloats
On its wild and tender notes.
     The morning red
     From yonder head   20
Sweeping down the mountain side
Past the pine trees in their pride
To the ravine's gullet wide
     Doth pursue
     The flying dew.

At last from the shroud
Of many a domed cloud
The sun rushes proud
    Of his restless fire,
    Wild with desire   30
To browse upon the dancing light
Of the moon whose sickle bright
Reapeth the barren night,
    On the steel-like flare
    Of her streaming hair.

23. *Pan*

I sing of Pan and his piping sweet,
 King of the shade and the sunlight
That dance amongst the flames of the wheat,
 I sing too of the dew bounding
From the impress of the steeds' feet.
 I sing of solitude,
Temple decked to Pan by that race
 Of mysterious priests
Who've seen the great god face to face,   9
 Who of Pan their melodious king
Have heard hushed talk among the leaves,
 Who have heard the brooks the story sing
How an angel race once lived on earth
 With bountiful Pan as their King.
A new god rose who hated man;
 They died, their shades possess the earth,
And to the woods fled bountiful Pan.

24. Child's Play

I know a merry thicket
It was never spoilt by man's care,
Tis a glad mad thicket
For no raked smooth paths are there
But thorn bushes wind all about
Thick with blackberries big sweet
Ground briars that literally shout
Soft moss all round my feet.   8

Also some four-footed things
A sleek rabbit neath a stump,
Also some things with wings
They nest in a hazel clump.
Not all there's a coot in a bank
Covered with grass that's rank,
Once a wood guest in a fir tree
Who would sit and blink and wink   16
Never stirred from his nest for me
Was too brave got shot I think.
Often I lie there on the moss and kick my heels
Dream and make believe
I am a trapper, I will tell you how it feels
Common things to leave:
I think and at once a trapper am
Then common things look strange   24

That tree stump becomes a wigwam
Red men the forest range,
Now I am called the white bear
For every one has a fine mane there,
Something wriggles to that bush near
You say a lizard I say a deer,
That noise the rustle of a meadow through the trees
No I say a prairie rolling in the fresh breeze,   32
Far beyond are the rocky mountains blue
And—but you laugh, I will tell no more to you.

25. *I sat upon a high gnarled root*

I sat upon a high gnarled root
Counting the songs of sap and fruit
When from a pine tree straight and tall
That grew amid my mountain dens
A small bird let some catches fall
As though he would some song recall
As is the way with wrens.   7
Then from the pines' eternal feet
To him I cried these measures meet:
"Peace be with you brother mine
Peace be with you golden crested
Peace unto you, somber breasted
Dweller in the tufted pine.
Whither is that song of thine
That bucolic wild of thine?   15
In some fay-delighting glade
In the soft and purple shade
That the mountain ashes made
By all other birds forgotten
Wast that song of thine begotten?"
Then the wren this answer made:
"In no fay-delighting glade
By all other birds forgotten
Was this song of mine begotten,   24
But when the great sun revelled high

And drunk the blood of hot July
I sought the woodland's sweet dominions
Where Zephyr sits with folden pinions
And the streams roll on in their mystic slumbers
Wearily beating their dulcet numbers,   30
Singing, singing, along
And the still leaves rejoice
As they fondle the voice
Of their sweet summer song."

Then a wonderful spirit arose
Out of the soul of a wild wood rose,
In its hand was a golden lyre
Every note was a quivering fire.   38
I trembled and gazed on his cold blue eyes
Whose light was the light of far away skies,
He sang me a song of primal things
A tale of the souls of ancient springs,
I think the wee wild fairy folk
In many hidden places
And in the hearts of pine and oak
Treasure the rhythmical paces,   46
But I am very sad when I think
As I sit here in the sun and blink
Mayhap 'twas nothing at all
Only the clarion call
Of a far-off water fall.

26. *The dew comes dropping*

The dew comes dropping
  O'er elm and willow
And soft without stopping
  As tear on pillow—
Yea softly falls
As bugle calls
On hill and dell
  Or liquid note
  From the straining throat
Of Philomel.   10
As the dew drops dart
  Each one's a thought
  From heaven brought
To the evening's heart.

27. *The Outlaw's Bridal*

Ireland 16—

Dost thou not fear an outlaw's mournful love:
To be always with him, young lowland daughter,
Who slew his brother by the western water,
A dweller with rivers on the hills above?
    Dost thou not fear an outlaw's cave
Where are no yielding pillows for thy head,
An outlaw's arms and heather for thy bed
    And in the end an outlaw's grave?   8

Dost thou not fear the tireless bandog's hate
Tracking our way by every sandy fountain,
Tracking our way along the heathery mountain,
Awaking to an undivided fate
    My steel-worn brows and thy soft head?
Dost thou not fear the tireless bandog's yell?
To pass from love to loveless heaven or hell,
    From dreams of dalliance to the dead?   16

And thou shalt fear him in each kiss and see
His slouching phantom in the golden morning,
And fear him when beside some pool adorning
Thy bodily form, to make it beautiful for me.
    Dost thou not fear, dost thou not fear
The mushroom-dotted grass at chilly Dawn
Where are no dolphined fountains, no smooth lawn
    And pleasant house to give you cheer?   24

Maiden, dost thou not fear a love so lone?
No eyes of friends to see thy soft hair flowing,
For they are dead my old companions—blowing,
Blowing the winds are through each white breast-bone.
    In dewy wood or on bare hill
The sword or arrow found them and they ceased.
The raven of their flesh has made a feast
    And the strong eagle taken his fill.   32

Yea, wilt thou have an outlaw's mournful love:
Then up, spring up before me on the saddle.
As I have ridden far, let Brian paddle
His tired hooves in the stream. I have thy glove
    Still on the fore of my steel cap.
But hark, dost thou not hear the bandog bay
Rolling among the hollows far away,
    Rolling along the mountain gap?   40

On! On! They overtake us. Leap thy best
Now Brian. Over the dark ravine thy furthest
Leap thou. Cling close belovéd, now thou earnest
Long days of love or an eternal rest.
    Kiss me lest thou should'st find the last.
We're safe. Hear how the great stones clash and fall
Below us from the ravine's ragged wall
    Clanging—we loosed them as we passed.   48

On—on—now are they miles and miles away.
Where the slow surges shoreward march we wander
Loose-reined along the grey sea sands. There yonder
I slew my brother; mingling in mere play
    Our swords, the fever of the fight
Fell on us and I slew. He was the first
And last of all my band. Now am I curst
    Of God by noon, and morn and night,   56

And all who go with me are ever lost
And pass out to the grave-world sorrow-laden,
And ah dost thou not fear God's curses, maiden?
Thine eyes give answer, my sad life wrath-tossed
    Thou sharest here in heaven or hell.
Cling close beloved that I may feel thy peace
Near to my soul where day by day increase
    The ever starless whirlwinds fell.   64

The sea sands pass. The gathering mountains close
Close gathering round us. Yon our pathway lieth,
The slow morn dawns. Our twisted shadow flieth
Along with us. The cloud-washed mountain goes
    Sheer to the plain a thousand feet—
Tread softly now, have I not called thee best
Of steeds and from great Brian named thee—West
    White Equinoxial billows beat.   72

Below the moonlight fits a forest's gloom;
Often above the thunder's roar and rattle
The war-god's talking of my land's long battle
Here where on man's worn spirit falls a doom
    Of sadness from the monstrous clouds
He is so near to, is our lime-stone cave,
Here will we live, far off from shield and glaive
    Far off from tedious warrior crowds.   80

28. *Love's Decay*

A riverside. A boat in the rushes. Two lovers awaiting the
    bugle's call that divides them.
        She
The giddy day goes barefoot on the hills,
She hath her scarlet slippers somewhere left
Within the chambers of the sky.
        He
                            And laughs
Teasing away poor night with globes of flame
From the deep woods. She hides for sleep poor thing,
The mother of sleep who knows no good but sleep
Within the lily's funnel and the folds
Of shadowy purple in the rose's heart,
In hanging foxgloves and the quiet river   10
And in the shadows of your spinning wheel.
        She
You like a lover gaze into her eyes,
What see you there oh wooer of night?
        He
The lure and mystery of things a-dying.
        She
Then look no more, my wooer of the night.
Ah gaze no more on her nor on the earth
The loneliest dewdrop in the midst of space,
The old and bitter earth has never loved,
Nor gaze along the wood its spirit loved
To madness in his youth and was deceived   20

And he is now all sighs. Gaze thou on me
And I will laugh and you'll be scarce so sad.
But ah, you're gazing on the wood and sky,
I loved them once but now I have no joy
Save only thee: the blue of yon kingfisher
Frets me—the useless fire.

     He

                       I have no joy
Save only thee: the blue of yon faint star
That holdeth her unending festival
In a wild songless melancholy waste
Is throbbing as a fever in my brain.   30
Oh dear one, lace thine hands across mine eyes
And I will see no more my wanderings
At thy young feet all restlessness hath died
And I could weave forever daisy chains
As children do their whole philosophy
To watch with solemn eyes the devious chain
Grow in the grass. I could well nigh forget
The lonely voice of yonder violet star
That sings how endlessly from star to star
The angels sweep, for them the burthen is   40
Of the eternal loneliness. Far down
Within the deeps, so sings the star, God broods
With rugged brows and never resting eyes,
Ere any world was born he rose from sleep
That no beginning knew and saw his loneliness,
And being filled with fear of the vast spaces
That had no voice and fear of his dread self

He snatched from his own spirit flakes of fire
And hurled them with a cry into the dark.
Thus angels formed he and talking worlds,   50
And bid them buzz away his loneliness
And mourns the voice of yonder violet star.
They are the tongues of his own loneliness
And such am I, these hands, thy glimmering eyes,
Thy lingering mouth, and all that moves and loves.
Oh lay thy fluttering fingers o'er mine eyes
My sweet, and I will cry the wild star lies.

    She

Star of the foam tossed up before my feet,
O would that none before us ever loved.

                    (A trumpet sounds.)

    He

Away my destiny.

    She

              Oh let me fix   60
This red rose in your cap I scarce can reach
You are so tall—so tall. How many girls
Have stood a tiptoe weaving roses round
False lovers' caps?

    He

             A thousand.

    She

                    More than that,
Ah more than that.

                    (The trumpet sounds.)

He

I cannot stay, farewell.

She (letting the rose fall)

Ah stay till I have perched the rose above
Your peaked cap. See where amid the shade
The soft rose shines. I'll pull another—thus!
And lay it gently down beside the first.
They are the shadowy eyes of maidens' loves   70
That had no voice and gazed away their life,
So when they died the pitying spirits bid
The roses be their musing eyes, and thee
And me they're watching now those envious souls
Through yonder crimson gaze—Kiss me beloved.

(The trumpet sounds.)

Ah heed it not, leave wandering for the waves
And for the winds that walk among the stars.

(He steps into the boat.)

She (slowly fixing the rose in his cap and bursting into tears)

You will forget me soon
Oh dear one hate me rather than forget.

*(The trumpet sounds; he pushes off into the river. On the far side a
procession of girls pass carrying a statue of the virgin and singing a
song.)*

Oh Mary keep the million hands of battle   80
Harmless as thine own hands when there go by
The young men or amid the ignorant rattle
Of dizzy war they may drop down and die
Before they live.

God gave the hawk for meed
To spring through voiceless caverns of the sky,
His spirit worn with suffering of speed
Immeasurable. Let him drop down and die
For he has lived.
          Rapture of alien laughter
Breaking the sloth of woods with many a cry
God gave the gypsy children and there after   90
Passion of wandering let them drop and die
For they have lived.
            God gave the salmon wary
The long and piping rivers lapsing by
As us the weary spindle—may they die
For they have lived.
   A Voice Singing Alone
Hear me oh mother Mary,
Let not my lover be mongst those who die
Our love's the youngest thing beneath the sky,
White Mary.

29. *Wherever in the wastes*

Wherever in the wastes of wrinkling sand
Worn by the fan of ever flaming time
Longing for human converse, we have pitched
A camp for musing in some seldom spot
Of not unkindly nurture, and let loose
To roam and ponder those sad dromedaries
Our dreams, the Master of the pilgrimage
Cries, "Nay—the caravan goes ever on,
The goal lies further than the morning star."

POEMS

OF

THE

1890s

30. *The Watch-Fire*

This song unto all who would gather together and hold
    Brother by brother;
A watch and a ward by the watch-fire of Eri, our old
    And long-weeping mother.

This song unto all who would stand by the fire of her hope,
    And droop not nor slumber;
But keep up the high and the mirthful proud courage to cope
    With wrongs beyond number.   8

This song unto all who would gather and help yet once more
    Eri, our mother;
And do nought that would anger the famous and great gone
  before
    Brother by brother.

31. *To a Sister of the Cross and the Rose*

No daughter of the Iron Times,
 The Holy Future summons you;
 Its voice is in the falling dew
In quiet star light, in these rhymes,
In this sad heart consuming slow—
 Cast all good common hopes away,
 For I have seen the enchanted day
And heard the morning bugles blow.   8

August
1891

32. The Pathway

Archangels were I God should go
   Unhook the stars out of the sky
   And in a sudden hurry fly
And spread them in a shining row—
A shining pathway as were meet.
   I had alone my life for thee;
   Tread gently tread most tenderly
My life is under thy sad feet.   8

August 5th
1891

33. *He who bids*

He who bids the white plains of the pole
  From His brooding warm years be apart—
He has made me the friend of your soul—
  Ah he keeps for another your heart.

October
1891

34. A Dream of a Life
Before This One

The cries of the curlew and peewit, the honey-pale orb of the moon,
The dew-covered grass of the valley, our mother the sea with her
croon,
The leaping green leaves of the woodland, the flame of the stars in
the skies
Were dearer than long white fingers, and more than your soft dark
eyes;

You came and moved near me a little, with tender, remembering
grace,
The sad rose colours of autumn with weariness mixed in your face,
My world was fallen and over, for soft dark eyes on it shone;
A thousand years it had waited, and now it is over and gone!   8

"You were more to me than a brother of old in the desert land."
How softly you spake it, how softly—"I give but a friendly hand:
They sold us in slavery together, before this life had begun,
But Love bides nobody's bidding, being older than moon or sun."

Nine ages ago did I meet you, and mingle my gaze with your gaze;
They mingled a moment and parted, and weariness fell on our days,
And we went alone on our journey, and envied the grass-covered
dead,
For Love had gone by us unheeding, a crown of stars on his head.   16

35. He treads a road

He treads a road of ghost and gleam
To please Him well my rhyme must be
A dyed and figured mystery,
Thought hid in thought, dream hid in dream.

36. On a Child's Death

You shadowy armies of the dead
Why did you take the starlike head
The faltering feet, the little hand?
For purple kings are in your band
And there the hearts of poets beat;
Why did you take the faltering feet?
She had much need of some fair thing
To make love spread his quiet wing
Above the tumult of her days
And shut out foolish blame and praise.   10
She has her squirrel and her birds
But these have no sweet human words
And cannot call her by her name:
Their love is but a woodland flame.
You wealthy armies of the dead
Why did you take the starlike head?

WBY
Sept 5
1893

37. *I will not in grey hours*

I will not in grey hours revoke
   The gift I gave in hours of light
Before the breath of slander broke
   The thread my folly had drawn tight,

The little thread weak hope had made
   To bind two lonely hearts in one
But loves of light must fade and fade
   Till all the dooms of men are spun.   8

The gift I gave once more I give
   For you may come to winter time
But your white flower of beauty live
   In a poor foolish book of rhyme.

March 10th 94

38. *Though loud years come*

Though loud years come and loud years go
A friend is the best thing here below.
Shall we a better marvel find
When the loud years have fallen behind?

Notes to the Poems

Abbreviations used in the notes:

CLI   *Collected Letters of W. B. Yeats,* vol. I, ed. John S. Kelly and Eric Domville (Oxford: Oxford University Press, 1986).

Early Poetry I   W. B. Yeats, *The Early Poetry, Volume I: Mosada and The Island of Statues,* ed. George Bornstein (Ithaca: Cornell University Press, 1987).

Early Poetry II   W. B. Yeats, *The Early Poetry, Volume II: "The Wanderings of Oisin" and Other Early Poems to 1895,* ed. George Bornstein (Ithaca: Cornell University Press, 1994).

E&I   W. B. Yeats, *Essays and Introductions* (New York: Macmillan, 1961).

MBY   Michael Butler Yeats.

NLI   National Library of Ireland.

Poems   W. B. Yeats, *The Poems* (revised), ed. Richard J. Finneran (New York: Macmillan, 1989).

POEMS OF THE 1880S

1.   *A flower has blossomed* (NLI 30439)

Yeats wrote these early lines on the back of a letter of 1882 to Mary Cronin, probably the wife of the solicitor Robert Barry Cronin, who was shortly to move from Dublin to Mitchelstown in County Cork. In the letter Yeats called the enclosed lyric (likely this one but possibly a different poem) the "shortest and most intelligible" of his poems and said that the subject "was suggested by my last two visits to Kilrock," a house in Howth occupied by the Yeatses' landlords Joseph and Sidney Wright. He added that "my great aim is directness and extreme simplicity" (*CLI* 6–7).

   4   Yeats may have written "meadow" instead of "measure."

   6   I have chosen the spelling "sacred" for the word that Yeats wrote as "sacret." It is possible that he intended "secret," but "sacred" seems the more likely meaning.

2.   *A double moon or more ago* (NLI 30338)

This early romantic lyric apparently refers to an unanswered question in a previous letter to an unknown correspondent, possibly the Mary Cronin of the previous note but more likely Yeats's distant cousin and early infatuation Laura Armstrong.

14   In his note to the poem "The Danaan Quicken Tree" (*Poems,* p. 535), published in *The Bookman* for May 1893, Yeats wrote that "It is said that an enchanted tree grew once on the little lake-island of Innisfree, and that its berries were, according to one legend, poisonous to mortals, and according to another, able to endow them with more than mortal powers. Both legends say that the berries were the food of the *Tuatha de Danaan,* or faeries. Quicken is the old Irish name for the mountain ash."

3.   *Behold the man* (NLI 30347)

This poem provides an early treatment of a favorite Yeatsian theme, the isolation of the exceptional individual. It is a semi-Petrarchan sonnet, with a couplet at the start of the sestet to result in a rhyme scheme of *abbaabba ccdeed.* Yeats signed the manuscript with his initials and dated it March 8, 1884.

1   "Behold the man" is, of course, the phrase that Pontius Pilate uses when he presents Jesus to the hostile crowd in the Bible (John 19:5), though Yeats may not have intended so specific an identification.

8   Dido is the legendary Cathaginian queen who falls in love with Aeneas (the "wanderer" of line 9) in Virgil's *Aeneid,* where he abandons her to seek the new home that the gods had promised him. Slightly reworked, these lines turn up later in Yeats's first major published work *The Island of Statues* (*Poems,* 453 and 481), which he began around the same time (*Early Poetry I,* 129).

4.   *Sir Roland* (NLI 30830, 30328, and 30440)

Partly in imitation of Spenser's *The Faerie Queene,* this early (probably 1884) knightly narrative is written in Spenserian stanzas, nine-line units rhymed *ababbcbcc* with the first eight in iambic pentameter and the last in iambic hexameter. Like Shelley, Spenser was a particularly important precursor for the young Yeats, who edited *Poems of Spenser* for publication in 1906 and reprinted its introduction as "Edmund Spenser" in his own prose collection *The Cutting of an Agate*. Yeats did not bring this poem to quite so finished a state as most of the others in the present volume, resulting in a less polished and occasionally obscure text.

14   In classical mythology, Lethe is the river from which shades drink in Hades to forget the past.

22   A Templar was a member of the Knights Templars, an order of knighthood founded in the early twelfth century to protect pilgrims en route to Jerusalem. Its growing wealth and political power aroused strong opposition from European rulers, and it was officially suppressed by the pope in 1312.

27   This line and line 29 are particularly difficult to decipher; see *Early Poetry II*.

37–45   Yeats apparently marked this stanza (#5) for deletion, along with the second stanza six (lines 55–63) and stanza seven (lines 64–72). I have placed all three of those stanzas within brackets to indicate apparent deletion, but have included them in the main text because by describing first the valley and then within it the old knight who will shortly take over the narration, they make the plot easier to follow.

109–17   Yeats also marked this stanza (#12) for deletion. I have placed it in brackets to indicate that, but have included it for its help in making the narrative more comprehensible.

114   The word "Within" began a phrase, "Within / The waters," continued in the next line. When Yeats canceled "The

waters," he left "Within" syntactically isolated at the end of line 114 (where it does fulfill the needs of rhyme).

124   There is an illegible word, indicated here by a bracketed question mark, before "hands."

127   Ingiborg (also Ingeborg and other variants) was a Danish princess who married the king of France in 1193. But given the description "Ingiborg the dead Norwegian queen" in line 171, Yeats more likely means the character in the Norwegian saga of Frithioth the Bold. A translation of that work by Yeats's early mentor William Morris first appeared in 1871.

180   At the top of the next page Yeats wrote, "When through the wind thy sweet name [? ?]," which he may have intended as a revision to stanza 19.

182   In Roman mythology Cupid is the god of love, the counterpart of the Greek Eros.

183   A psaltery is a stringed musical instrument, but Yeats presumably means "psalter," which refers to the Book of Psalms and, hence, in Roman Catholic ritual a series of 150 sentences or aspirations commemorating certain mysteries. The literal manuscript spelling is "phasaltery."

198–99   The manuscript has two stanzas numbered "21."

211   The manuscript may read "beast" instead of "breast."

231   This section of the manuscript (NLI 30328) breaks off here at the bottom of a page. The remainder of stanza 24 is missing, as are stanzas 25 and 26. The text resumes with NLI 30440, which begins with stanza 27.

237   Sansloy (Lawless), like Sansfoy (Faithless) in line 245 and Sansjoy (Joyless) in line 262, is a figure in the first book of Spenser's epic *Faerie Queene,* where he opposes the Redcrosse Knight.

267   Although this version of the poem is marked "END" after this line, Yeats used similar material on other occasions. The two stanzas below, which appear with the manuscript of "Sir Roland," are not fully Spenserian in form (the first has seven rather than nine lines, and the second breaks off in the middle of line 8), but they resemble the concluding stanzas of "Sir Roland" in subject, diction, and tone. They are written with ink and paper similar to those of the main poem and may be part of an alternative draft.

28.

Low hums the wind and as the smoky rings
Fall ring on ring from kindling watch-fires heart
And light wherewith dumb nature speaks and sings
Pours forth—so humming from the wind's soul start
Sound rings on rings and withering depart
Unto the cavern high with fluttering flight
The word arose—yea speech is nature's spoken light

29.

"Sansloy my name is and all chains I hurl
Afar for fain would I free-pinioned seek
Joy's footing on the sea or where the merle
Goes through the shadowy woods with flutings weak,
And I have asked all things that shine or speak,
The glow worms and the old owls in their trees,
Where dwelleth Joy by mere or mountain peak
Or sea but

5. *Sansloy—Sansfoy—Sansjoy* (NLI 30440)

This three-stanza medievalizing lyric exists in a fair copy manuscript currently included with leaves containing the final stanzas of "Sir Roland" and the additonal stanzas cited above in the note to line 267 of "Sir Roland." Its diction, imagery, and theme clearly resemble the conclusion of the longer poem. For the figures of its Spenserian title (Sansloy or "Lawless," Sansfoy or "Faithless," and Sansjoy or "Joyless") see the above note to line 237 of "Sir Roland." At the end of the lyric Yeats dated it "Sept[ember]," presumably 1884.

6. *The Priest of Pan* (NLI 30446)

"The Priest of Pan," not to be confused with the different poem "Pan" also included in this edition, shows the influence on the young Yeats of Elizabethan and Romantic Hellenizing. In Greek mythology Pan is the god of flocks and shepherds, and hence sometimes of nature in general. Images of fountains, rural escape, and secret wisdom would reappear throughout Yeats's career.

    8   In Greek mythology, oreads were nymphs associated with mountains and caves.

7. *The Magpie* (NLI 30449)

Yeats wrote this four-stanza love lyric on a single leaf of paper folded in half, and he signed it at the end. The poem provides an early example of his lifelong fondness for eight-line stanzas, which came to fruition in mature poems of varying rhyme schemes, such as "Sailing to Byzantium" or "In Memory of Major Robert Gregory." Yeats's punctuation for the dialogue in the last four lines of each stanza was fragmentary and inconsistent, with resultant instability of the text. While the system followed here seems the most appropriate, other choices would yield differently punctuated texts inviting slightly different interpretations. The interested reader may consult the manuscript evidence in *Early Poetry II*.

8.   *'Mong meadows of sweet grain* (NLI 30454)

The draft of this little lyric about a poet and a brook is written on paper watermarked 1884 and was presumably composed about the same time. It may have been intended as part of a play.

9.   *I heard a rose on the brim* (NLI 30458)

This version of "I heard a rose" appears to be a slightly later reworking of a song in the first act of the unpublished early play variously referred to as *The Blindness, The Equator of Wild Olives,* and *The Epic of the Forest*. It dates from between 1883 (the date of the watermark) and 1886, when Yeats finally finished tinkering with the drama. The lyric owes a debt to Blake, particularly to "The Sick Rose" from *Songs of Experience,* and anticipates some of the poems that Yeats would later collect as *The Rose* and *The Wind Among the Reeds.*

4   Yeats may have intended "prattling" instead of "prating"; the manuscript reads "pratting."

10. *Hushed in the vale of Dagestan* (NLI 30459)

Dagestan (also Daghestan) is a region in the eastern Caucasus, on the Caspian Sea. This poem is based on one called "The Dream" by the Russian poet Mikhail Lermontov. The dying figure here anticipates the more fortunate Irish hero of "The Outlaw's Bridal," below.

Lines 2–4 originally read:

> *I lay and lead was in my side*
> *Up from the wound the blue smoke ran*
> *Down from the wound a bloody tide.*

4   Yeats may have written "coiled" instead of "curled."

12   Yeats first called the tale "eager," then apparently "wondrous," and finally "lisping."

11. *For clapping hands* (NLI 30823)

This lyric sounds an early instance of the typical Yeatsian romantic theme of the poet standing apart from social applause or appreciation. It is written on paper watermarked 1884 and was probably composed that year or the next. The draft appears on one side of a single leaf of paper, with an earlier version of the opening lines on the back, and it is possible that the poem continued on another, now lost leaf.

6   In the manuscript the second word of this line reads "though," presumably in error for "thou."

8   Yeats presumably intended "wrapt" as "wrapped," but in his wayward orthography may have meant "rapt."

11   This line of the manuscript is heavily revised and the resultant reading necessarily tentative.

12.   *An Old and Solitary One* (NLI 30826)

This early rondel-like example of Yeatsian aloofness appears on a leaf of paper with two quatrains (one of them published in both "In a Drawing Room" and "Quatrains and Aphorisms") on the verso. The paper is watermarked 1882 and the draft of the quatrain appears earlier than its publication in *Dublin University Review* for January 1886.

13–14   In both these lines, the word transcribed as "when" may be "where."

13.   *The Veiled Voices and the Questions of the Dark* (NLI 30829)

Yeats originally titled this early sonnet "A Rime Democratic" before canceling that title and replacing it with the present one. The poem is written on paper watermarked 1883 and was probably composed during 1883–84. It is one of Yeats's few early poems set in a modern city, with the speaker in this case riding a tram car.

3   A Pharisee was a member of an ancient Jewish sect that emphasized strict observation of both written and oral Mosaic law; in derogatory Christian usage the term has overtones of hypocrisy and self-righteousness.

14.   *A soul of the fountain* (NLI 30832)

This embryonic dialogue poem blends Yeats's interest in English poetry and in Oriental themes, with the admonition to "be bold" coming from Spenser and the diaphanous veil image perhaps from Shelley. The last stanza anticipates Yeats's more mature vision of cycles. The poem probably dates from the early or middle 1880s.

3   By Abeysherd Yeats may mean Abu Shahrain, the modern Iraqi name for Eridu, the earliest known city of Sumer.

6–9   The "ancient book" is likely Spenser's epic *The Faerie Queene,* where in Book III Britomart encounters the house of Busirane. In stanza liv of canto XI there she reads the inscriptions above the doors: *"Be bold, be bold,* and euery where *Be bold"* and *"Be not too bold."* The passage was a favorite of Yeats, who included it in his edition of *Poems of Spenser* (1906).

16   In Yeats's early dramatic poem *Mosada* (1886), Azolar is described as "the star-taught Moor" (*Poems,* p. 492).

18   The last two words of the line are particularly difficult to decipher and hence partly conjectural.

15.   *Cyprian* (NLI 30839)

Cyprian's monologue exemplifies well Yeats's early interest in dramatic poetry. Although the manuscript labels this speech "Scene 1" and identifies Cyprian as speaker, the rest of the play is not known and may never have existed, with the monologue being a free-standing poem in its own right. Its themes of rebellion, isolation, and the lake-girt island all reflect Yeats's early interest in Shelley, while the use of classical mythology is typical of his poetry before he met John O'Leary in 1885. In *Yeats: The Man and the Masks* (New York: Norton, reprinted 1979), p. 32, Richard Ellmann says that Yeats wrote these lines "in the middle of his eighteenth year."

9   Zeus was chief of the Greek gods, who dwelled on Mount Olympus.

10   Although the poem is set in Classical times, the account of the "robber nation" causing men to weep for ages may suggest England in its relation to Ireland.

21   In Greek mythology, oreads were nymphs associated with mountains and caves.

16.   *My song thou knowest* (NLI 31042)

The address to his art, medieval or renaissance setting, and romantic diction are familiar elements of Yeats's early work. This five-line poem is preserved in the same manuscript as a draft of the poem "Love and Death" published in *Dublin University Review* for May 1885, and probably dates from 1884 or early 1885.

17.   *The world is but a strange romance* (NLI 12161)

This poem and the next eight are found in an album of both bound and loose leaves with a dark blue-green cover with gold trim. It is difficult to look at the golden bird on the cover of this early notebook without wondering if it provides one of the many sources for the more famous golden bird in Yeats's great mature poem "Sailing to Byzantium." For period of composition, the fact that some of the pages are watermarked 1882 provides the earliest possible date, though 1883–84 seems more likely and even 1885 possible.

"The world is but a strange romance" is written inside the front cover of the notebook and provides a sort of introduction to the collection. Yeats inscribed it within a decorative sketch of bluebells, a butterfly, and a body of water, and signed it "WBY."

7   hairbells (also harebells) are bluebell flowers.

18.   *The Old Grey Man* (NLI 12161)

This provides yet another example of Yeats's early and life-long fascination with inspired poet-figures, here the old grey man who also assumes the demeanor and function of a bard (or skald). The long hair of the maiden, the conjunction of silver and gold, and the presentation of vision all recur in Yeats's later work.

19.   *The Dell* (NLI 12161)

"The Dell" occupies the top part of a manuscript page and "Inscription for a Christmas Card" (poem 20 in the present edition) the bottom part. It is one of Yeats's earliest poems with a fairy reference; the bees, honey, bow, and flowers would likewise recur in his verse.

20.   *Inscription for a Christmas Card* (NLI 12161)

This is the third and longest draft of this poem found in the album. After its initial reference to a "time of holly," the poem leaves its seasonal subject behind and returns to Yeats's normal early literary concerns. The unrhymed last line may indicate that the poem is incomplete. "By" in line 3, "call" in line 6, and "shouting" in line 17 are particularly conjectural readings.

21. *Tower wind-beaten grim* (NLI 12161)

Yeats could occasionally be whimsical or humorous in his poetry, and this poem offers a good early example of those moods.
Wind, tower, and ghosts, of course, would become major images
in his later work, especially in regard to the opposition between
natural and supernatural.

22. *Sunrise* (NLI 12161)

This expression of natural energy and desire rates among the
most technically polished of Yeats's unpublished work of the
1880s. The poem's five-line units, alternating three rhymed te-
trameter lines with two of dimeter in an *aaabb* pattern, frequently spill over metrically and syntactically. The reference to
"elf or gnome" in line 7 presages the Irish turn that Yeats would
shortly take, in contrast to the classical invocation of Proserpine
in line 11.

11   In classical mythology, Proserpine (or Persephone) was
the daughter of Zeus and Demeter. In some accounts she was
carried off to Hades by Dis, and thus became associated both
with the underworld and with rituals of agricultural fertility.

31   Yeats may have written "daring" rather than "dancing."

23. *Pan* (NLI 12161)

This poem has an exceptionally full compositional record. At
least nine separate drafts survive, each with revisions or alter-
ations, thus making a total of eighteen different stages of the

poem's evolution. The version transcribed here is the most advanced one and originally ended with the following lines, which Yeats canceled:

> *Ere he fled he cast forgetfulness*
> *On all, for he loved and pitied man,*
> *   But a few he called to follow him.*
> *In this temple of perfect beauty*
> *   He tells them strange and wonderful things*
> *And he ~~teaches~~ prepares them to prophesy.*

The interested reader will find the entire record in *The Early Poetry II.*

The poem itself provides an early example of Yeats's lifelong cyclical view of history, here with the civilization associated with Pan being displaced by that of the new god, whose hostile attitude toward mankind appears to be the opposite of Pan's beneficent one. In Greek mythology, Pan is the god of flocks and shepherds, and hence of nature in general; invention of the shepherd's pipe was ascribed to him.

4   "bounding" is a tentative reading; the manuscript is particularly difficult to decipher there.

24. *Child's Play* (NLI 12161)

This appears to be one of the earliest poems in the album and marks an important phase in Yeats's youthful poetic development. He recalled it with typically wayward spelling in a letter of 1889 to his friend the Irish poet Katharine Tynan:

> *My ideas of a poem have greatly changed since I wrote*
> *the Island. Oisin is an incident or series of incidents[,]*
> *the "Island of Statues" a region. There is a thicket*
> *between three roads, some distance from any of them,*
> *in the midst of Howth. I used to spend a great deal of*
> *time in that small thicket when at Howth. The other*
> *day I turned up a poem in broken metre written long*
> *ago about it. That thicket gave me my first thought of*
> *what a long poem should be, I thought of it as a region*
> *into which one should wander from the cares of life.*
> *The charecters [sic] were to be no more real than the*
> *shadows that people the Howth thicket. There [sic] mis-*
> *sion was to lesson [sic] the solitude without destroying*
> *its peace. (CLI 135)*

21   The passage about the trapper may recall the lines about
the "old hunter talking with gods" from Browning's early poem
Pauline. There Browning treated two subjects that also obsessed
Yeats, his reading and his relation to Shelley. Yeats alluded to
the Browning passage throughout his career, most memorably
in the late poem "Are You Content."

33   I have left "rocky mountains" in lower case as a general
reference, but Yeats may have intended more specifically the
Rocky Mountains in the American West.

25.   *I sat upon a high gnarled root* (NLI 12161)

"I sat upon a high gnarled root" is the last poem from the early
album transcribed in the present edition. In general structure as
a woodland vision and sometimes in specific phraseology (like

that of the last three lines) it has similarities to "The Old Grey Man," while as an early verse dialogue it anticipates "Love's Decay" (transcribed below) and Yeats's many published dialogue poems. Birds, of course, were among Yeats's favorite symbols throughout his poetic career.

34   It is difficult to tell exactly where the wren's song ends. I have followed here the most likely solution, but the manuscript's irregular and overfrequent use of inverted commas, combined with the scantiness of its other punctuation, would allow for other choices. Indeed, the manuscript text concludes with a quotation mark.

26.   *The dew comes dropping* (NLI 30752)

This tripping lyric provides another instance of Yeats's early treatment of nature as sympathetic rather than antithetical to human life and emotion. The reverse side of the manuscript contains a pencil sketch labeled "Laying foundation stone of Museum in Kildare Street" in the margin and "H. R. H. In Ireland—1885" at the bottom.

10   Philomel (or Philomela) and Procne were two daughters of Pandion, king of Athens. Pandion's ally Tereus, king of Thrace, first married Procne and then raped Philomel and cut out her tongue to ensure silence, but she wove her story into a piece of embroidery that she sent to her sister. In Greek accounts the gods changed Procne into a nightingale and Philomel into a swallow, but most English authors follow the reversal in Latin tradition by which Philomel becomes the nightingale.

27.   *The Outlaw's Bridal* (NLI 30456)

This ten-stanza narrative poem reflects Yeats's turn to Irish materials and settings in his poety after meeting the aged Fenian John O'Leary in 1885. It preserves some of the atmosphere of "Hushed in the vale of Dagestan" but transfers it to seventeenth-century Ireland. Although Yeats's subtitle "Ireland 16—" is chronologically broad, he may have had specifically Cromwellian times in mind. His related poem "The Protestants' Leap" was published in *The Gael*, of which O'Leary was literary editor, and the present work may have been intended for the same journal. Although the outlaw has inadvertently slain his brother, his reference to "my land's long battle" suggests a nationalist dimension to his predicament. The fusion of nationalism, eroticism, and a solitary hero wondering if his beloved will forsake the world for him recurs frequently in Yeats's later poetry.

9   "Bandog" originally meant a fierce dog tied or chained up, hence a mastiff or bloodhound.

71   Given the other Irish references in the poem, the name "great Brian" suggests Brian Boru, the famous high king of Ireland in the Middle Ages.

80   Immediately after this line in the manuscript follows a draft of Yeats's lyric "A Faery Song" (first published in 1891) written in a different ink and with a device of a circle with an "x" through it separating that lyric from the poem transcribed here.

28.   *Love's Decay* (NLI 30066)

This dramatic poem provides an early example of Yeats's dialogue poetry, which would later feature speakers like "Hic" and

"Ille" in "Ego Dominus Tuus" or "The Soul" and "The Heart" of the seventh section of "Vacillation." Here the conjunction of star, boat, and lovers owes something to Yeats's reading of Shelley. In his essay "The Philosophy of Shelley's Poetry" (1900), Yeats identified his predecessor's characteristic vision as "a boat drifting down a broad river between high hills where there were caves and towers, and following the light of one Star" (*E&I* 95). The poem's concluding procession of girls invoking Mary seems more a generalized religious reference, possibly medieval, than a specifically Irish one.

A canceled line in the manuscript made the psychological situation more specific than it appears in the final version: "He is faithless to her and to his cause. She suspects perhaps." The manuscript itself appears on loose leaves contained in a black notebook. Like the other materials in the notebook—a song from *The Island of Statues* and a draft of the opening lines of *Time and the Witch Vivien*—"Love's Decay" probably dates from 1884–85.

29.   *Wherever in the wastes* (Huntington Library)

This nine-line poem is contained in a letter from Yeats to his friend the poet Katharine Tynan, dated June 25, 1887, and continued on July 1. I concur with the judgment of John Kelly in *The Collected Letters of W. B. Yeats, Volume One* that the poem was "probably composed by WBY for the occasion." Tynan has left several amusing accounts of the early Yeats in her autobiography *Twenty-five Years,* including one of him reciting Shelley's "The Sensitive Plant" during a rainstorm instead of holding the umbrella properly. "Wherever in the wastes" still remembers

Shelley in its final image of the morning star, but also resembles Arthur Henry Hallam and, of course, Edward Fitzgerald's version of the *Rubaiyat* of Omar Khayyam.

POEMS OF THE 1890S

30. *The Watch-Fire* (Yeats Library, Anne Yeats)

This three-stanza patriotic poem survives only on a scrap of proof paper in the collection of Anne Butler Yeats, the poet's daughter. It presumably dates from the early 1890s, when Yeats also published his poem on the death of the nationalist leader Charles Stewart Parnell, "Mourn—And Then Onward," in the newspaper *United Ireland* for October 10, 1891. The two poems together represent Yeats's closest verse approach to the nationalist rhetoric of Young Ireland, which Yeats admired for its ability to reach a wide audience but criticized for its lack of both sophisticated technique and emotional subtlety.

Title: In an interview published in the *Irish Theosophist* in fall of 1893, Yeats spoke of a desire to publish "a collection of essays, and lectures dealing with Irish nationality and literature, which will probably appear under the title of the 'Watch Fire.' "

3   Eri or Erin is an ancient name for Ireland, frequently figured as a woman.

31. *To a Sister of the Cross and the Rose* (NLI 30318)

This poem and the next two come from a carefully assembled manuscript album covered in yellow cloth in black stitching and inscribed "W. B. Yeats. / 'The Rosy Cross.' Lyrics." The six poems in that collection are dated variously from August to November 22, 1891. As he did with his published books, Yeats apparently meditated the sequence of poems carefully. Here is their arrangement in *The Rosy Cross:*

1. *Untitled (later published as "A Song of the Rosy Cross")*
2. *A Salutation (later published as "He Tells of the Perfect Beauty")*
3. *To a Sister of the Cross and the Rose*
4. *The Pathway*
5. *Untitled ("He who bids the white plains of the pole")*
6. *Untitled (later published as "A Dream of Death")*

Very similar versions of the three unpublished poems reproduced in the current edition also appeared in the overlapping manuscript collection *The Flame of the Spirit,* a full vellum notebook that Yeats presented as a love token to Maud Gonne on October 20, 1891. In addition, a more mystic version of "To a Sister" appears in the more casually assembled white manuscript album MBY 548, which contains drafts of various Yeats poems of the early 1890s, especially those that appeared in his book *The Wind Among the Reeds* (1899). For more information on the three collections, and for verbatim transcriptions of pertinent parts, see *Early Poetry II.*

Title: The title combines the Rosicrucian elements of Rose and Cross appropriate to the Hermetic Order of the Golden Dawn, an esoteric society that Yeats had joined in March of 1890 and that he induced Gonne to join in the autumn of 1891.

Previously, they had both belonged to the Theosophical Society, whose doctrines also pervade the poem. Gonne would thus likely be the *soror* or "sister" addressed in the title, though Yeats characteristically avoided naming her and thus limiting the poem's range of potential reference. Yeats variously associated Rosicrucian elements with a range of interpretations, including esoteric doctrine, erotic longing, suffering and desire of various kinds, the poetic imagination itself, and even nationalist inspiration.

1 "Iron Times" refers to the myth of a former Golden Age and its return, in contrast to current decline into an Age of Iron, as set forth for example in Virgil's "Fourth Eclogue" and redacted in Shelley's final chorus to *Hellas,* both of which Yeats drew on for "Two Songs from a Play."

32. *The Pathway* (NLI 30318)

In *The Rosy Cross* manuscript album (see above, poem 31) this poem follows immediately after "To a Sister of the Cross and the Rose" and, like that lyric, combines erotic and esoteric meanings. A very similar version called "Your Pathway" appears in the *Flame of the Spirit* manuscript collection as well, where it is dated July 5, 1891. In *The Rosy Cross,* Yeats crossed out "July" and substituted "August."

33. *He who bids* (NLI 30318)

"He who bids" comes fifth in *The Rosy Cross* manuscript collection, immediately after "To a Sister" and "The Pathway." It perhaps voices Yeats's frustrated love for Gonne more directly than the preceding poems. He had proposed to her unsuccessfully again in July 1891; Gonne had been having a secret affair with Lucien Millevoye, a follower of the French general Boulanger. The very similar version for *Flame of the Spirit* begins in the past tense ("He who bade . . .").

34. *A Dream of a Life Before This One* (Beinecke Library, Yale University)

This poem got as far as being set in page proof for *The Countess Kathleen and Various Legends and Lyrics* (London: T. Fisher Unwin, 1892) before Yeats canceled it, possibly because of its overly explicit reference to a dream of Gonne's. As Yeats wrote in the draft version of his autobiography,

> *I was not, it seems—not altogether—captive; but presently came from her a letter touching a little upon her sadness, and telling of a dream of some past life. She and I had been brother and sister somewhere on the edge of the Arabian desert, and sold together into slavery. She had an impression of some long journey and of miles upon miles of the desert sand. I returned to Dublin at once, and that evening, but a few minutes after we had met, asked her to marry me. I remember a curious thing. I had come into the room with that purpose in my mind, and hardly looked at her or thought of her beauty. I sat there holding her hand and speaking vehemently. She did not take away her hand for a while. I ceased to speak, and presently as I sat in silence I felt her nearness to me and her beauty. At once I knew that my confidence had gone, and an*

> *instant later she drew her hand away. No, she could*
> *not marry—there were reasons—she would never*
> *marry; but in words that had no conventional ring*
> *she asked for my friendship. (Memoirs,* ed. Denis
> Donoghue, London: Macmillan, 1972, p. 46)

On the Yale proofs, Yeats changed the title from "Remembrance" to "A Dream of a Life Before This One." An earlier version of the poem appears in *The Flame of the Spirit* album, where it is titled "Cycles Ago" and subtitled "In memory of your dream one July night." Yeats would have found the idea of cycles and ages in Classical, English poetic, and esoteric traditions, including Virgil, Blake and Shelley, and Madam Blavatsky.

8   Yeats's correction of the proofs would have resulted in the unlikely phrase "and now it is over gone" at the end of the line; I have inserted "and" for the sake of sense and meter.

13   Nine is a recurrent number in esoteric lore. Yeats knew about historical cycles from many sources and eventually produced his own conception of historical ages in the "Dove or Swan" section of his book *A Vision*.

35.   *He treads a road* (MBY 548)

Two drafts of this poem appear in the white manuscript album MBY 548, which also contains drafts of the remaining three poems printed below here, together with drafts of other work, much of which subsequently appeared in *The Wind Among the Reeds* (1899).

1   The earlier draft of this line begins "God loves the road" rather than "He treads a road."

2–3   Compare "my rhyme must be / A dyed and figured mystery" here to "a song should be / A painted and be-pictured argosy" in lines 4–5 of "Sir Roland" (poem 4, above) nearly a decade earlier.

36.   *On a Child's Death* (Woodruff Library, Emory University)

This moving lyric commemorates the death of Maud Gonne's illegitimate child Georges, who died of illness (probably meningitis) on August 31, 1891. Although she at first led Yeats and others to think that the child was adopted and sometimes even that it was a girl, the boy Georges was born in early 1890 to Gonne and her lover, the French political journalist Lucien Millevoye. At the time of the death, Yeats still did not know that Gonne was the child's birth mother. Her sorrow at the death and belief in occult forces led Gonne to try to reincarnate Georges's soul through intercourse with Millevoye in the child's burial vault, an effort that resulted in the birth of their daughter Iseult on August 6, 1894. This version, transcribed into Lady Gregory's copy of Yeats's *Poems* (1899), appears to derive from the most advanced of the three versions in the MBY 548 album and, like that one, is dated September 5, 1893.

9   The "tumult of her days" suggests Gonne's political activism, which Yeats saw as leading her away from tranquil personal love.

11   "her squirrel and her birds": Gonne was fond of animals, and often appeared in public and even traveled with various of her pets.

37. *I will not in grey hours* (MBY 548)

This three-quatrain poem accords with many of Yeats's other love lyrics of the time. Although he does not mention Maud Gonne specifically, it is possible that the "breath of slander" refers to attacks on her. Both the first and third stanzas of the manuscript contain alternate readings.

1   "revoke" replaces an earlier reading "retake."

3   The line earlier read "Before a slanderer's touch could break."

10   A brace pairs "may" with the alternate reading "will."

12   A brace pairs "a" with the alternate reading "this."

38. *Though loud years come* (MBY 548)

This quatrain appears at the bottom of a page also containing a draft of "A Poet to His Beloved," later published in *The Wind Among the Reeds.*